Visit us on the Web!
StepIntoReading.com
rhcbooks.com

Educators and librarians, for a variety of teaching tools, visit us at RHTeachersLibrarians.com

ISBN 978-0-593-37566-2 (proprietary edition)

This special edition was printed for Kohl's, Inc.
(for distribution on behalf of Kohl's Cares, LLC, its wholly owned subsidiary)
by Penguin Random House LLC.

KOHL'S
Style Number JHD1-5525
Factory Number 208840
Production Date 10/2020

MANUFACTURED IN CHINA
10 9 8 7 6 5 4 3 2 1

DreamWorks Trolls

The Sound of Spring

by David Lewman

illustrated by Character Building
and Fabio Laguna

Random House 🏠 New York

It is a warm spring night
in Trolls Village.
All the Trolls are sleeping
except one.

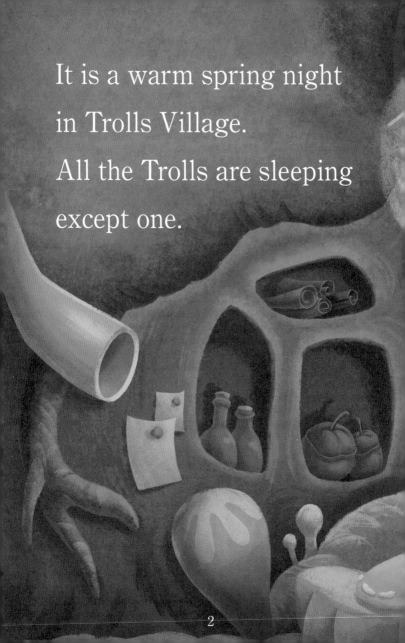

Branch is wide awake.

He hears something.

What's that sound?

It sounds like chirping.
Is there a bird
in the house?

Branch looks around.

No bird!

In the morning,
Branch still hears
chirping.

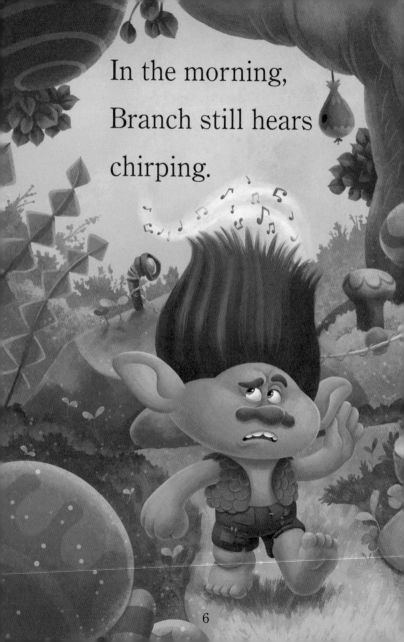

6

He checks the village.
He cannot find
what is making
the sound.

The chirping is driving him crazy!

Branch asks Cloud Guy
if he hears the sound.
Cloud Guy listens.

He hears
the chirping, too.
He asks Branch
if *he* is making the sound.

Branch says no.
Cloud Guy says
Branch *must*
be chirping!

11

Branch says,

"I am *not* chirping!"

Branch thinks Cloud Guy

is playing a trick on him.

He is angry.

He chases Cloud Guy

through the woods!

Poppy sees her friends.
She asks them
what's wrong.
Branch tells Poppy
about the chirping.

14

Poppy listens closely.
She knows where
the sound
is coming from!

Poppy reaches into
Branch's hair
and pulls out an egg!

That is where
the chirping
is coming from!
A bird must have laid
an egg in Branch's hair!

17

Poppy says the egg
is about to hatch!

A bird comes out
of the egg.
It sings a song.
Poppy and Branch
sing, too!

The little bird's
mother hears
her baby singing.
She comes right away!

They fly off together.

Everyone waves goodbye.
Branch misses the bird's
chirping a little . . .
but not *too* much.